Up to the Toys

Written *by*:

Sis and Mis

Up to the Toys

Copyright © 2021 by Sis and Mis

Printed in the United States of America

Content

Chapter 1

The I and His Creation

I T WAS A TRULY PERFECT DAY until it wasn't. It arrived without warning, just as they had planned. It wasn't a tidal wave of change, more like a tsunami. The waves broke on every aspect of daily toy life. Businesses closed, schools closed, stay-at-home orders were issued, as were mandatory mask wearing, indoctrination of children, shortages of goods, emptying of store shelves, and rising death tolls. Toys were pitted against each other, and faith was under fire. Fear controlled Toy Planet. Life existed in the twilight zone, somewhere between the pit of their fears and the summit of knowledge they were being given. The unknowing was debilitating.

Light glistened off the ocean waves as if sending a message in Morse code. A distress signal was being relayed. Dot, dot, dot, dash, dash, dash, dot, dot, dot, three flashes of reflection off the water, three long flashes, followed by three short again. Nannymom had been observing this from her lounge chair on that beach for hours while soaking up some vitamin D. She watched intently as a message seemed to transmit across the waters as she meditated and pondered the question of what her purpose was in this life on this planet. How would The I use her life for the good of the Toy Planet and serve others?

The creator of the toys and everything on the planet was simply referred to by the toys as The I. The I loved watching over them and relished seeing them happy and productive. There was nothing The I would not do for them. The I had desired for them to be perfect.

When Nannymom's precious grandtoy Mercury had had her first seizure within two days of receiving five Inoc during a well toy office visit, Nannymom had started to ask questions. She had not been aware of it being a standard practice to give a toy that many Inocs at once or what the risks were. She hadn't given it a thought to even ask the doctor they trusted with Mercury if the Inoc was a good idea or created a high risk. Wishing she could turn back time and know what she knew today, she watched the waves roll and crash into the shoreline, creating a thick white froth that was churning sand. The waves made powerful, thunderous noises as they collided with the beach.

Nannymom could feel the tiny salty droplets adhere to her skin as she wandered along the sandy wet edge that the tide had recently left behind. There were smooth patches along the otherwise rough shore, which was composed of millions of crushed seashells worn by the waves crashing into the rocks. The shells appeared as though they had been run through an inefficient coffee bean grinder, leaving odd-shaped pieces behind. Their colors reminded Nannymom of a watercolor painting bleeding together: beige, white, gold, and different shades of purple. Walking along the shore in bare feet proved difficult with the sharp-edged bits of shell. She dodged from side to side to find a smooth spot on the sand. These smooth zones were a welcome contrast to the jagged edges. The random jagged edges pressing against the soles of her feet could not put a damper on the calming influence of the ocean.

Suddenly, Nannymom had an epiphany. What had happened to Mercury should never happen to another toy. As a legacy to her dear Mercury, Nannymom's life purpose would be to do everything in her power to prevent other toys from being injured by the Inocs. She had tried to quiet her thoughts, the guilt eating her up inside.

"I should have asked more questions. I should have asked to see the Inoc inserts and warnings. Maybe if I had asked for the risks of the diseases they were Inocing against the risks from the Inocs themselves. She hadn't even realized how many more Inocs had been added to the schedule and how many were being given to the new toys in such an early, short span of their lives. She knew so many of these toys could be saved with testing and research.

Nannymom began to pray to The I. "Use me, teach me to know how to help The innocent toys. The time is now. Help me protect the next generation of toys. Help me to save a whole generation of toys from being injured." She simply could not possess the wisdom she had acquired about Inocs and what was planned and not heed the call.

The seagulls communicated as they glided so close to the water's surface that it seemed as though a fish might stick its head out at any moment and be sucked down the bird's quick closing beaks. The sun was giving the earth its gifts of light and warmth.

The toy boats and ships floated on the ocean's horizon as if they were weightless. They looked so far away, yet they were within two miles of the coastline. So small and so vulnerable, they rode the rough waves that were fighting to carry them to shore.

Young and old toys strolled along the shore as their plush animated pets frolicked beside them. They absorbed all that The I had bestowed upon them. They unknowingly meditated to the sounds and feelings of peace that The I had given them.

The I was unhappy when they made choices that caused themselves pain and suffering and then found a way to blame Him. The I had done nothing but create a space of joy and love for them that was intended for the toys to grow and learn, to gain wisdom, and to help each other survive and thrive on this beautiful planet.

The creator wanted to tell the toys that it was time to make better choices, but He wished to give them more time to figure it out on their own before they caused themselves too much harm. The toys didn't recognize how much power they had of their own to find their own peace. They were designed to manifest anything they wished. The I did not tell them what to believe and gave them the free will to determine right from wrong.

The I marveled at how the toys had come up with so many different stories about their creator over the generations. They were making up new stories all the time and new ways to view The I. Curiously, most of the new stories materialistically benefited the storyteller. They kept building bigger and bigger buildings in The I's name, even knowing The I was everywhere. Ironically, it was the Mama Therez doll, who didn't even have a building, who understood exactly what The I had wanted.

There were so many interpretations and teachings of what The I had done and why. Who The I was, and most importantly, what The I expected from the toys. Sadly, all The I really wanted was to be loved by the toys and for them to be joyful and loving to each other. All the toys believed emphatically they were taught the right story of The I. What The I had noticed about the toys' stories was that most of these teachings followed the same rules and commandments, yet none of them were perfect. None on Toy Planet had a monopoly on The I, who longed for them to respect each other and how others' groups chose to love.

It was a blessing to love The I, and the toys felt that. They often thanked Him for all the good in their lives. The toys were able to call out to the creator when the toys needed help the most. Nannymom intuitively knew it was time to ask for The I's guidance. The toys had a relationship with The I, and they felt His power and presence in everything when they were open to His love. When they felt His immense love and calming energy, the toys then were inspired to share that love with each other. The I was the light, and without Him, it would grow dark. They didn't all have to see The I through the same lens. As long as they felt, shared, and enjoyed His love, all was peaceful and well.

Toy Planet was truly an exquisite creation. A world where the toys could live in unity with each other and be bound by love. The stuffed pet animals had no fear of the toys. For many years, The I was so proud of the harmonious nature the toys had created for themselves and for each other. All toys had their own space to call home, land to be cultivated safely, freedom to barter with their neighbor, and the opportunity to travel anywhere on Toy Planet. Toys were respectful and understanding of themselves and others, curious about everything, and protective of stuffed animals and nature. They worked together for the progress of Toy Planet because the toys had come a long way. They had created one nation, under The I, with liberty and justice for all.

Toy Planet was inhabited by a diverse collection of toys; some toys were wooden, others plastic, and many were metal. Whether they were shiny or dull, every toy had a unique and different size and shape. No matter what they looked like, the toys realized that their survival depended on resolving differences peacefully and getting along through compassion and care. The only laws the toys had were fundamental to providing a safe place for everyone to live.

The toys sang an anthem to remind themselves of their daily responsibility to uphold the well-being of everyone on Toy Planet:

Do no harm to one another. Love your sister and your brother.

No killing and no wars. Use your gifts and do your chores.

Toys don't judge, only love. We protect all gifts from above.

Knowledge is completely free. Sharing is what toys do for thee.

Telling lies is taboo. Toys don't lie. Toys love you.

Chapter 2

New and Better Toys

The toys enjoyed this peaceful paradise for many years until some new toys were manufactured. These new toys had shiny pieces that looked foreign to the other toys. The newly created were dissatisfied with the way things were on Toy Planet and believed themselves superior to the other toys. They thought they were smarter and stronger and knew exactly what was best. They believed they deserved more than the other toys because they were modern and technologically advanced, engineered with blinking lights and computer chips. It was because of this attitude that these self-avowed Illuminated toys were determined to run Toy Planet better than how The I had created it.

These Illuminated toys so strongly believed in their ideals that they formed a union to change the society of Toy Planet completely. They met up in a secret toy castle and devised a plan to do exactly that. Because of their advanced computer chips, The Illuminated toys understood they had to avoid telling the other toys about their plan; the less complex, vintage toys wouldn't understand the benefits of doing so. They also knew that these standard toys were satisfied with their lives the way that The I had ordained it to be.

They devised a plan to sow discord amongst the toys so that they would start to believe that things weren't really so good and could certainly be made better. Better for whom was the question they hoped the toys would never ask. The Illuminated toys set to work, convincing the toy masses that they need not work so hard to have the things they wanted. It was a simple plan to be used on what they believed to be simple toys. Planting seeds of doubt was an integral part.

"Was it fair that some toys had so much and that it came so easy for them?"

"Shouldn't all toys have the latest gadgets?"

"Didn't they deserve it?"

The new Illuminated toys were brilliant in their understanding of the simpler toys. Apathetic, fatigued toys don't fight back. But this would not be enough to completely change Toy Planet. The logic chips within the upgraded toy brains told them this. The common toys had faith in The I and trusted the plan of The I, so this faith had to be destroyed. The toys needed to doubt how they were created and to question The I's love. They couldn't be allowed to join together and worship The I. Fellowship only strengthened their faith... the faith the Illuminated toys wanted to be placed in them.

And finally, for their takeover of Toy Planet to succeed, the Illuminated toys needed the other toys to believe that they were fragile beings that could be easily torn, broken, and diseased. They needed all toys to depend on them for their cures to everything. This way, they could alter the toys and make them weaker with time without them even realizing it.

Weaker toys could be controlled and wouldn't question those who said they would make their lives less strenuous. And most importantly, weak, damaged toys wouldn't create so many new toys. The enlightened didn't appreciate so many of Toy Planet's resources being used by lesser, undeserving toys. Since there were so many useless, outdated toys using up Toy Planet's resources, the Illuminated needed a way to eliminate many of them quickly and efficiently without the other toys ever realizing that they were being destroyed on purpose. The Illuminated toys could promise that everything the standard toys needed would be handed to them and that they would be taken care of by the stronger, more enlightened toys.

The first thing on the Illuminated's list of priorities was to keep the toys distracted, which would ensure they wouldn't have a chance to truly communicate with one another. Otherwise, they might figure out what was going on and attempt to stop it. Toys fighting among themselves would never figure out who their real enemy was. A small percentage of toys would resist the changes, and all they had to do was make these resisters look foolish to all the other toys so that they wouldn't be taken seriously.

The Iluminated toys had no reservations or guilt about what they were setting out to do.

Weren't they created superior to other toys for a reason?

Didn't they deserve more and better because of this?

Was this not their ultimate destiny?

The Illuminated were designed to be the ruling class. Certainly, they were... and all the Illuminated agreed.

So, on a chilly night, in an ancient and portentous castle that had been built by toy soldiers centuries before for the old money wealthy Rothbots and Rocketellers, the Illuminated toys met. This evil, egocentric group sat in luxurious brocade wine velvet wing-backed chairs around a cozy fire, being waited upon by the old butler, Alfred Nickelsworth, and the maid, fondly referred to as "Nannymom."

Alfred Nickelsworth and Nannymom had been trusted servants, having been with the family for as long as anyone could remember. They were antique toys and made of nothing but cotton, leather, and a few buttons. The Illuminated believed the servants wouldn't even be able to comprehend the ins and outs of the Illuminated plans.

However, Nannymom had easily comprehended the evil, unemphatic, narcissistic, sociopathic plan they had been devising. So, while they chatted away, Nannymom was making mental notes of her own.

The leader of the ruling class was Sir William Hates. He was a truly magnificent toy who could change forms with the click of a button. He had lithium batteries and a highly advanced computer chip that allowed him to communicate and move about freely, no remote control necessary. He was top of the line in toy creation, so it only made sense that he was appointed the chairman of the Society of Illuminated Toys. Being naturally analytical, he was never concerned with the feelings of the other toys, so it was easy for him to devise a plan to control even those who also sought control.

Along with Hates, five other toys were invited to the castle. First was Robobot Eugene Ickes, who was designed to be cute while being deceptively clever. He had all-terrain tracks in place of feet that allowed him to travel over many different surfaces without difficulty, which the other toys greatly admired.

Astrobot Noah Better, who came from a long assembly line of advanced engineered toys, was naturally narcissistic. Like Robobot Eugene Ickes, Astrobot Noah Better loved the idea of ruling the other toys.

Also invited to the castle was Lord Hasmore, an older toy who had been created without the computer chip, which automatically made him lesser than the other members of the Illuminated, but since he was part of a long line of successful toys, he was included out of necessity. Lord Hasmore and his family owned much of the toy media and manufacturing; both were essential to control if the Illuminated toys' plan was to succeed.

The next member of the society was Lord Geno Syde. He was created with a wealth of accessories that allowed him to engage in different coveted activities. He had toy horses, toy cars, and even came with toy airplanes. The only thing missing in Lord Geno Syde was a soul processing chip, which allowed empathy for the other toys.

Last was Lady HellenorBot, who was a masterpiece of creation. She had been built to have a sleeker appearance than the other bots. She had a glittering silver metallic finish on her mechanical arms and legs and large glass blue eyes, which allowed her to stealthily track anyone or anything. She had a gold antenna on her head that permitted her to pick up radio signals and play them through a speaker located inside her chest. A very sophisticated computer chip was installed within HellenorBot that could process several streams of information simultaneously. She was very quick and advanced with her responses, which made her more intelligent than all other toys.

These six toys, who truly believed they were superior to all the others, sat comfortably together around the castle's fireplace, sipping on syrupy sodas. Led by Sir William Hates, they devised a plan that stealthily tracked anything or anyone. After much discussion into the late hours of the night, a plan unfolded.

"Sheep can't think for themselves, so the wolves will always control them." That was Robobot Eugene Ickes's favorite quote. "It's a simple law of nature," he added. "Whether you call it Social Darwinism or by another name, the result never changes. There is no need to feel bad about it. This is the way it was meant to be."

"But," he reminded the other five Illuminated toys, "don't fool yourselves. The masses like it this way. The standard toys don't really want to have to think for themselves. It is much easier to hand the control over to some toy who is more advanced and capable. That is why we are such a gift to Toy Planet." Robobot Eugene Ickes smirked at that last statement. The other toys were looking at him like he was much more than a toy now, and Robobot Eugene Ickes loved it.

Astrobot Noah Better chuckled when he thought about how the masses believed that those in control had their best interests in mind. He really was an inherent tyrant, and he took pride in that fact. There was no question that the "sheep," which he referred to as anyone who was not illuminated, deserved their fate. Astrobot Noah Better learned most of what he knew about control and manipulation from his grandfather, who had recently expired at ninety-nine years old. The old toy's batteries had leaked acid and damaged him beyond repair. His logic processor, though, was as sharp as the day it was manufactured. Grandfather Astrobot Neverenuph was created during a different era, but they shared a similar vision. He loved to recall his participation in the failed attempt to "organize society," as he referred to it.

"And we would have triumphed, had they listened to me!" he would shout suddenly, sitting upright in his wine velvet chair (the same chair that Robobot Eugene Ickes sat in now), shaking his brass-headed mahogany cane in frustration. "We had everything right here!" And he would place his wrinkled fist in the palm of his other hand. "Right here!" he emphasized as he beat his fist against his palm. "This could have all been laid to rest decades ago." He always added this statement as he collapsed back into his chair.

Astrobot Noah Better relished in these memories, being at the family estate and listening to his grandfather who had lived through so much. Grandfather had taken part in the first attempt at world control. Yes, it had failed, but they had learned so much from that failure. Lessons that Astrobot Neverenuph taught his grandson, to avoid another failure. They now knew that a military takeover was unlikely to succeed. They understood that the masses could not appreciate the commonsense eugenics plays in creating a better society for every toy.

Eugenics was the science of improving a toy population through controlled design to increase the occurrence of desirable characteristics. Developed as a method of improving the toy population, it fell into disfavor only after the perversion of its doctrines by its creators. Grandfather had explained how the Third Realm had been a dictatorship where nearly all aspects of life were controlled by government. However, none of that was important now. Though the Hollowcost had failed, the Fourth Realm would triumph in engineering an organized society. It was a brilliant understanding of psychology, propaganda, and manipulation of the trusting nature of toys that would allow the Illuminated Elite toys to control the fate of Toy Planet.

Astrobot Noah Better thought back on a memory of a conversation he'd had with his grandfather years ago.

"Grandfather?" a younger Astrobot Noah Better gently said, so as not to startle his dozing grandfather. It was very warm in the drawing room, seated next to the beloved large stone fireplace. Fire crackled and popped and filled the room with the scent of burning wood with undertones of caramelized brown sugar. The flames offered an eerie flickering light. While

Grandfather's mind was still intact, his old body was drained of energy. He often sat with his eyes closed, so one couldn't be certain if he was listening or not.

"Yes, my dear toy?" he replied.

"It wasn't a complete failure. You and your comrades did succeed in controlling the information and education introduced to the masses," Astrobot Noah Better said, looking up at the old man seated across from him as he rolled his candy cigar between his fingers.

Grandfather perked up quickly at the mention of this. "No, no, of course you're right. The first attempt of control did provide the future leaders with a good foundation. We learned from our mistakes. You know, Noah, it was much easier to run experiments then. I don't know when toys became so fickle. Now everything must be hush-hush or under the guise of something else. Such nonsense." Everything that slowed Grandfather down or got in his way was "nonsense."

There were many lessons to learn and hurdles to overcome, following the trials that were conducted at the end of the Third Realm. A "toyatarian" code had been written after those hearings by the do-gooders. Twenty of the twenty-three defendants were doctors who had been involved in the toy experiments and mass destruction of toys under the guise of euthanasia. Millions of toys had been discarded in the toy bin. The Third Realm had used their best doctors and scientists in their original experiments. Grandfather laughed out loud at the number one code as he read it. "The voluntary consent of the toy subject is absolutely essential."

These do-gooders had brought the Third Realm's toy soldiers, scientists, and doctors to trial, and they had collaborated on the construction of a set of ten new rules to stop further abuse and experimentation of toys across the planet. Grandfather had known they could have easily found a way to circumvent the toyatarian codes of scientific experimentation; they would make their experiments "mandatory, not voluntary."

"Although, I must admit, it's been much easier than I had anticipated when we originally devised the plan to enlighten society after the war," he said. Grandfather had many years ago learned to choose words for effect. Words had power; the Furor had taught them that well. The Furor had been a very articulate, artificial intelligence toy that had been pivotal in the elimination of scores of innocent toys whom he believed were inferior to the other toys. He saw them as defective even though they weren't.

He created wars between the toys and caused destruction the toys had never seen. The toys had vowed they would never let it happen again. Grandfather and his Illuminated friends no longer spoke of an "organized society" in public, which Grandfather was brought to understand after the war had negative connotations to the foolish masses. Now, whenever the ultimate goal was spoken of, it was to create an "enlightened society." Who wouldn't want to live in an enlightened society?

"You weren't alive yet, my dear boy, and your father was still a pile of metals and processors. Oh, how I wish you could have been amongst those of us in that first planning committee after the war ended. It took place right here in this very room," Grandfather said, his eyes sparkling like a real-life doll's at the mention of the memory. "We laid out everything in detail. We left nothing to chance this time. Members of our faction were sent to every country. If we controlled the Intele-tele, then we find a way to circumvent it. Never underestimate the power of propaganda, Astrobot Noah," he said, looking the young toy straight in the face.

He had made this point many times before, but repetition had a lot of power. "Back then, we had newspapers and radio, but it was the Intel-tele that really got things moving. We made sure every home got an Intel-tele. For years, that was our strongest way of influencing public opinion. We had the computers, but they weren't at a place yet to be carried in every single pocket like they are today."

At this, Grandfather chuckled. "I have to admit we had plans and contingency plans, but a computer that could listen to everything that every toy on the planet says, can influence their thoughts, and can track them anywhere at any time?! Even we could not have planned this until a few decades ago. Toy control has quickly gotten easier and easier. It wasn't as easy to influence toys in the early days. There were still a lot of independent thinkers at that time; they questioned everything and trusted nothing that wasn't proven to them. A smart lot they were, before we became better at programming them, that is. We knew we were going to have to deal with them some other way, or they'd get wise and could cause us grief. There are things I seriously doubted we could ever achieve, but we not only have achieved them but also have surmounted them in my lifetime. We are almost at the goal, and no one besides the elite toys, the top one percent of the toy population, and a few outliers in the masses even realize it. There is nothing that can be done to stop us now."

Nannymom poured Grandfather another syrupy soda as she managed a contrived smile.

Astrobot Noah Better had admired his grandfather. His death was a great loss to the enlightenment movement, but he was determined to complete the work started by Grandfather and the others of the Third Realm. He would make his Grandfather Neverenuph proud.

The Great Reject had been set into motion. This time, all the older, sicker toys would be rejected. A virus was created that would create fear and panic in all the toys while targeting and eliminating all the toys who had become dependent and were causing a strain on the economy of Toy Planet. How would they explain a virus that only killed this social class of toys? They wouldn't have to. They would just isolate and cause division amongst the toys so that they wouldn't be able to communicate or come up with their own strategies to interfere with the Great Reject.

How brilliant that while this was being accomplished, the younger toys were being reprogrammed to support their plan and be assets to them in the future. They were clueless to the freedoms they were relinquishing, which their forefathers had died for, when their last plan had failed. The younger toys were being fed information that was being censored to only contain content to support the plan and maintain confusion among the toys. None of the toys could agree on what was actually happening; so cunningly diabolical was the plan. It was seemingly overnight that they were infiltrated, manipulated, and easily controlled by the fear of bringing harm to one another.

The Illuminated Toys created their own commandments for the toys of Toy Planet to replace that silly anthem the toys insisted on singing.

These Ten Commandments for Toys (so all toys could be happy and healthy) were ordered and decreed:

1. **All parents of new toys must allow their toys to be Inoc'd on the schedule, dictated by the Toy Planet Health Organization.**

2. **All parents must be repeatedly Inoc'd to prevent getting ill or passing illness onto the younger toys.**

3. **If any toy feels they are not joyful in all things, that toy should be sent to see the Nutcracker for the appropriate gummy pills. All toys should be happy at all times, no matter the circumstances.**

4. All toys are encouraged to borrow more monopoly money from the pig bank. This is to ensure that all toys have their latest dream house, dream car, and dream vacation. There is no need to be struggling when there is monopoly money!

5. All toys must be supplied with the latest Wokey-talkies and Intele-teles. Let's stay connected!

6. All toys, to maintain good condition, must adhere to the food triangle and eat several servings of Carnagrub and drink several servings of Carnacream daily.

7. Any toy that complains of any kind of distress must take the prescribed properly colored gummy pill given to them by Dr. Didsolittle for the prescribed length of time. Not doing so could lead to serious toy defects. The doctors always know best.

8. All information provided on the Intel-tele and Wokey-talkies by the Squeaky Toy Media is factual and should not be questioned.

9. All toys must listen to the Toy Planet Health Organization's advice on social distancing, masking, isolating, closing businesses, and anything else they deem necessary for toy safety.

10. **All toys must join either the Donkey Party or the Elephant Party and fervently, even violently, defend the beliefs of their party and their land.**

This group of Misleaders knew their endgame: total control. They created the new set of commandments to replace what the toys had recognized as their commandments from The I. Just as Grandfather Neverenuph once did, the Misleaders planted all the necessary seeds for their deceitful garden to grow. Over time, the wealthy gained more power, which created the perfect storm for the Misleaders. Since these bots and their families started buying the pill plants, the pig banks, and the Intel-tele stations and started taking control of the Toy Health Organizations, the Misleaders' influence became more and more pronounced.

At this point, the Misleaders and those affiliated controlled ninety percent of the monopoly money. They could gradually convince the masses that these new commandments would lead to better lives for them and their families. The ruling class would protect them and care for them. They also had connections and common interests with many of the clowns who ran the government, so influencing them would be a piece of cake for these cunning bots.

There were toy factories all over Toy Planet, but the biggest factory was in Stuffed Eagle Land. When the Misleaders finally took control of that factory, the factories that hadn't been acquired yet by the Misleaders would fall like dominoes. They already pulled the strings on the puppets that "ran" the toy factories. They were full of their own fluff and loved to hear themselves speak.

The Misleaders weren't as smart as many toys believed them to be. Most of what they did was just for show and to justify their positions of power. The Illuminated toys knew this and used the Misleaders' egos against them. The Illuminated toys knew they'd cut the strings off these puppets when the takeover was complete.

And for the final blow, Sir William Hates's ultimate plan was creating toy illnesses. Illnesses that Dr. Didsolittle would not be able to cure. If you couldn't cure it, at best, you could Inoc against it to "protect" everyone in the toy community. This was brilliant. They would turn Healthcare into Wealthcare. It would create a steady stream of income for the pill plants, which the Illuminated owned and operated.

For years, there had been warnings that advances in toy science could make it possible to create toy plagues. "This is just one example of what modern technologies can do," noted Dr. Fallacy, a very famous toy doctor. Toy scientists, watching the rapid advancements in synthetic biology, feared it was only a matter of time before the obstacles to creating viruses from scratch were surmounted. Dr. Fallacy was the head scientist on these studies because no one knew more about dangerous, contagious diseases than him. Obviously, this made it necessary for Sir William Hates to have him on his side. He needed Dr. Fallacy's expertise on the most powerful weapon they would ever need.

Members of the Toy Planet Health Organization had warned the committee that the science was there, and there could be nothing good to come out of these synthetic biology studies. Heated debates in Stuffed Eagle Land about this research occurred. Most notably was the threat of rogue agents with deadly knowledge on how to weaponize pathogens. Dr. Fallacy said he did not think the work would have received the green light in Stuffed Eagle Land, so the research was done in a very northern region of Toy Planet and privately funded. There were many wealthy toys who gladly supported advancements in this line of science. They considered themselves visionaries.

The Toy Planet Health Organization clearly listed mercury as one of the top ten poisons of major public health concern. But the Misleader-controlled scientists were dancing toys, so they did what dancing toys do: they danced around this fact and put it in the Inocs.

Furthermore, they had a backup: the metal aluminum. In truth, they knew the pretty silvery shiny metals would slowly build up in the toys' systems, causing more and more harm until they would eventually have to be discarded in the damaged toy bin. Wasn't this the goal? Certainly, but the effect was slow and insidious, and the simplest toys would never make the connection. The toys would at first develop vague symptoms: fatigue, rashes, tummy troubles, foggy thinking, sadness, anxiety, withdrawal from others, toy bodies attacking themselves, and a plethora of other symptoms and infections. All symptoms that could be blamed on other causes and treated with many gummy pills.

The toy doctors, who directly cared for the toys, were taught that toy bodies holding on to the silvery metals was such a rare occurrence that it wasn't even worth testing for, so they should not do so even if the sick toys asked for this test. Just to be safe, the Misleaders joined with the toy health security companies that were paid to control toy healthcare costs. The toys paid them to cover healthcare costs, and the Misleaders guided them on what to cover, and more importantly, what *not* to cover. The Toy health security agencies were happy about this; medical care was money, and the less they had to cover, the more money they made. The heads of these agencies, so they could sleep at night, reminded themselves of their responsibilities to shareholders. Less payout, more profit.

The dancing scientists knew mercury killed everything, so it kept costs down to combine the Inocs with mercury. They knew that aluminum scrambled toy brains and was toxic to their internal wiring. That was the purpose of "**preserves**," wasn't it? The Inocs could easily be separated and made safer without mercury or aluminum, but that would defeat both purposes— making money and creating sick toys. Therefore, the dancing toys continued to dance around the facts.

Many of the toys remembered a time not so long ago when Toy Planet was in danger from self-professed elite toys. Those were dark times. No one liked to think back on those horrible memories; however, they did recognize the value of learning from their mistakes. They had vowed to never lose their freedoms again. It was in giving up those freedoms that they had almost lost themselves. It was when they had turned against one another.

Despite many remembering this dark period, it was happening again. It looked and felt different this time, but slowly, they began losing their freedom of choice and speech. While toys naturally loved all other kinds of toys, that's not what the Infobots were reporting on the Intele-tele or ToyNet. The toys were confused by the Information they were receiving. Who were these toys who hurt their own kind? Wasn't it a toy commandment that they love each other? There was no way they could have known that what they were seeing was not real. Yet, they felt it was not real. They didn't personally know anyone that hated other toys, but the Intele-tele said it was happening all over Toy Planet. This truly disturbed the loving hearts they had.

These loving toys could not conceive this weapon that was being used to divide them, nor could they imagine the next weapons used against them would be disguised as something that would save them. Their minds were being altered, and their beliefs eroded a little at a time. They did not fathom they could be made sick, diseased, damaged, and dependent on Wealthcare forever, or that the young toys would be sterilized with the prick of a pin, which was supposedly used to create a "safer" world for "healthier" toys.

Chapter 3

The Misleadership

The guidance of the two-party system was when the real tragedy began. These parties were competing for power over the toy factories so they could control the money and the toys, their most prominent powers being the ability to pass laws and to raise monopoly money. Taxes were placed upon the movement of all toy money.

If the toys made money, they paid tax on it. If the toys spent money, they paid tax on it. It was a brilliant plan for those in government to have a massive stream of monopoly money. It was common knowledge that all those who were elected to government office left very, very wealthy. Billions in monopoly money were spent to get "elected" to office, but those in power knew it was money well invested because the rate of return was exponential.

Laws were slowly added to control the toys more and more and limit what the toy masses could do about it. Control of the toys was vital to their long-term plan. The Misleaders were supposed to represent the toys, but over time, they seemed to only represent and benefit a handful of toys. Most toys did not have someone in the toy factories looking out for their best interests.

The Misleader Leader from the Donkey Party happened to be a soft toy puppet named Jackass. Jackass worked in favor of liberal issues and for the lobbyists who had paid to have him elected to office. The Misleader Leader from the Elephant Party was an oversized stuffed puppet named Captain. He worked in favor of conservatism and for the elite lobbyists who had paid to have him elected to office. In truth, both were having their strings pulled by the Illuminated toys.

All day long and in every form of media, the Misleaders worked on misinforming the simple toys who had "elected" them. They spent millions and millions of monopoly money trying to prove that the other party had committed some type of crime. They strived to prove that the other was not credible and could not be trusted to have the toys' best interests at heart. Both party leaders had done unethical things to win that power. The party leaders said a lot of nice things, but when you looked just beneath the surface, you could find cracks in all the stories they told. Most toys did not want to put the time and effort into looking through the cracks. Life was too busy. Nowadays, the toys had plenty of things to distract them from the real problems. That, of course, was part of the Misleaders' plans.

So many things were promised during election season. Jackass promised to fix the economy and solve long-term problems such as healthcare, climate change, and the stimulation of more technology and innovation. Of course, all the promises did not get fulfilled. Captain vowed to repeal the latest healthcare act, make no cuts to social health programs, allow health security to cross state lines, blah blah blah. Once again, he did not fulfill this.

The toys were so fed up with it all. They had become apathetic to the whole production. All the two parties seemed to be successful at was causing division among the toys. There was so much animosity between the two parties that, eventually, this distrust and hatred spread amongst the toys. Divided toys would never be able to fight back. This was a very critical element to ensure the success of Sir William Hates's plan.

Misleaders' messages were broadcast to toy dream cars, the Intele-tele, and on all toy communication devices. Most of the information they received came from the elite Lord Hasmore. He was brilliant at designing propaganda. It was very hard to decipher who was telling the truth, or if the messages contained any truth at all. Twenty-four hours a day, the toys were bombarded with misleading information. The I had never intended this hatred to spread, but as mentioned previously, The I had given the toys the freedom to figure things out for themselves.

At this point, most of the toys had chosen a political side. They were either liberal or they were conservative. But for the most part, none could really explain why they had chosen their position. There was such pressure to pick a side. So many of the issues that were endlessly debated were never solved. The same list of problems was discussed for decades: toy migration, toy gummy pill abuse, toy healthcare, the cleanliness of Toy Planet, the best fuels for toy cars and homes, blah blah blah.

Most toys had figured out long ago these issues had uncomplicated answers, which is why they became apathetic to the messages played endlessly. There were messages day and night, night and day, that left the toys feeling unsatisfied, unsettled, and divided. It was as if the Misleaders never truly wanted to solve a problem or allow the toys to have peace and serenity. It was obvious they had their own agendas. Misleaders wanted control over the toys' lives, health, and monopoly money.

The pig bank was the center hub of monopoly money; those who controlled the pig bank controlled Toy Planet. They had lent them monopoly money that the toy calculators assured them they could afford until the poor, over-extended toys couldn't. Then, the pig bank would take all the homes back. Yet, when the pig bank got in trouble for creating this big bubble, they got to keep the toys' money and the piggy bankers got big bonuses.

All toys knew that bubbles were supposed to be fun, but now it seemed only the clowns in charge enjoyed bubbles. The clowns that ran the pig bank appeared to work hard at coming up with policies and projects aimed at helping the toys, but at the end of the day, the bulk of the funds benefited themselves. They were stealing the toys' dreams that they worked very hard to achieve. This had the effect of casting shadows over everything good. It made life for the toys feel like a struggle, and Toy Planet became a dark place where only those with power could thrive.

Despite all the monopoly money being printed, many toys were forced to live outdoors with no shelter. These toys were quickly injured by exposure to the wind, rain, and cold. The clowns reveled in the sorrow as they enjoyed their own overflowing wealth, status, and power.

On Toy Planet, toys knowing your name was also power. You could look all their names up on ToyNet and find out what they were worth. Twenty-two hundred toy families had a combined wealth of nine trillion dollars. There were even two toys who were worth a trillion dollars by themselves. Half of Toy Planet's wealth belonged to the top one percent of the toys. The top ten percent enjoyed eighty-five percent of the wealth, while the bottom held the remaining fifteen percent, to be shared among roughly eight billion toys trying to survive.

The disparity was unimaginable. It was hard to believe how bad things had gotten, without the toys even realizing how horrible things really were. There had always been those who had more, but nothing like today. Many remembered there being laws to prevent this from happening. They remembered laws to stop the monopoly money from being concentrated in the hands of the few. Weren't the Misleaders in the government responsible for making sure this never happened?

Some wondered how the billionaires lived. Toy Planet now had roughly twenty-two hundred billionaires. Most toy families lived on sixty-eight thousand monopoly dollars a year. This number represented the average household income on Toy Planet. How many houses, yachts, servants, etc. did the monopoly billionaires have or need? They had so much play money that most toys did not have.

The wealth imbalance of Toy Planet was not what The I had wanted for the toys. The I had wanted the toys to create a utopia, a place where no toy starved or went without what they needed.

Billionaire toys traveled the world, built compounds to protect themselves from the common toys, flew in private jets, bought gameball teams, took advantage of the best toy doctors to get the best stitching, took possession of Toy Planet's beaches, and figured out how to fly to Mars once they had destroyed Toy Planet. Meanwhile, other toys went without the basic needs. Why did these toys need millions and billions at the expense of the planet and their fellow toys?

Billions could have been spent on research to see why the young toys were getting sicker, on healthier food and lifestyle education, wellness care, and detoxifying the planet. What the simple toys didn't know was that in most cases, the toys would have been healthier if that they could avoid the healthcare being offered to them. Their healthcare money was being gobbled up by the pill plants that were creating many of the billionaires.

Robobot Neverenuph, Lord Hasmore, Lady HellenorBot, Sir William Hates, Astrobot Noah Better, and Robobot Eugene Ickes continued to acquire more for themselves and the rest of the one percent at the top. Less and less trickled down to the simple toys. And while it wasn't being shared, it was creating poverty, hunger, desperation, sickness, and sadness. This was part of their ultimate plan to control the simple toys.

The I knew what was happening and could have done something about it. He was waiting patiently for his beloved toys to learn their lessons and become truly enlightened. He knew they were smart enough. He knew they had the compassion to stand up for themselves and one another. He knew they loved each other. He knew they would find a peaceful way out from the suppression of the organizations. There was always one toy created who would speak the truth and lead the other toys to freedom. Nannymom cried out to The I, "Show me how to save the toys! Use me! This little light of mine, show me how to let it shine!"

Even the Misleaders would be enlightened one day. They weren't just robbing their fellow toys of joy; they were robbing themselves. What kind of life were they creating? The Misleaders had become so arrogant that they were destroying their own planet.

To make matters worse for the weak toys, the Misleaders financed and promoted energy sources they knew made the toys and the planet sick. They continued to provide this dirty energy due to the money it made and added the bonus of making so many toys weak and damaged. The wealthy were very careful to live in areas of the planet that were not affected by the fallout of filthy by-products of energy creation and were certain to filter their air and water.

The Misleaders even created and sold food that would gradually make the toys weaker. The simple toys would never link the illness back to diet. Not even many toy doctors did this. They had no conscience when it came to making profits, as long as they maintained power over the weak toys and kept their numbers in check.

When anything got in the Misleaders' way, they created wars. They themselves never fought or died in these wars. The children of the toys did. Those children were, of course, paid and convinced they were dying for a noble cause.

There really were too many toys on Toy Planet. There wasn't room for many more. Fewer toys meant a better world for those who remained. One hundred and fifty million toy children were living in poverty on Toy Planet without access to education, healthcare, housing, nutrition, sanitation, or water. Fewer toys meant better living conditions for those who survived and much better living conditions for the one-percenters. The Misleaders knew their work must be continued. They had come so far. They focused their efforts and resources on creating new Inocs.

Inocs were the solution to the population explosion.

Chapter 4

How the Toys Became Addicted and Apathetic

G I Jay was a tall, dark, curly-haired, dimpled, Italian thirty-year-old veteran toy soldier working in the oil fields when his doctor offered him OxyCotton Candy for his sore back in exchange for railroad ties to landscape his yard and pool area. Before long, Jay's Oxy prescription wasn't sustaining him through his doctor's office visits, and he resorted to buying stronger candy on the streets to satisfy his addiction. He overdosed after a failed rehab stay, leaving behind two beautiful children and a loving wife.

Lolo Abraham was a childhood star teen idol doll with a melodious voice and a great future. But the pressure to perform led her to seek relief and comfort in the form of gummy pills and sniffing powders. After just one year, they consumed Lolo, and she was sent to multiple rehabs in an effort to get clean. The joy of fame and fortune finally eluded her.

Katydid, a butterfly fairy doll capable of flight, grew up with a mother who gladly guided her to addiction. Her momma saw nothing wrong with gummy pills. The doctors gave them out, and they always made her feel better. What harm was in that? She had been selling the pills for Dr. Didsolittle for as long as Katydid could remember. She was able to help her family have nice things by selling gummy pills to some toys who needed them on the street. Katydid's momma never imagined that her child's life would end from her struggles with gummy pills that she herself had provided. She blindly trusted Dr. Didsolittle, and it ended up costing Katydid her life.

Many toy doctors did just what the pill plant representative wanted them to do. The representatives presented fancy slide shows to the doctors and educated them on the benefits their pills offered. To the doctors, it really seemed that what the pill plant reps were telling them about the new gummy pills was too good to be true, but why would they lie? Pill plants were in business to find cures for toy diseases, weren't they?

It was just by coincidence that most toy doctors were stuffed ostriches and stuck their heads in the ground when questions like these arose. After all, their pockets were full due to all the bonuses they received from the pill plants and the health security companies. The health security companies paid them for every Inoc they gave; the higher the number of Inocs, the more monopoly money. Besides, the ostrich doctors told themselves they were helping to take away the toys' pain and sickness. They sat all day long in their crisp white coats, under their oath to do no harm, passing out pills about which they knew very little.

The pill plants educated them on what pills they would like to sell the most and which pills they should prescribe to the toys the most. The new pills were always better than the old pills, even if the old pills had worked. Over half of the toys on the planet now had a pill bottle. Even though the doctors saw the death rate of toys increase, they didn't stop giving out the pills. They had the knowledge to care for the toys and make them well, but that would take time. They would have to go through the history of each toy, run many tests, and do a lot of work in follow-ups.

Time was money. It was so easy to just give their patients pills and send them on their way. This made the hospitals, doctors, and pill plants happy and money at the same time. Everyone accepted this fact except old Dr. Hippo. That old, wise, caring stuffed hippopotamus had created the Hippo Oath for toy doctors to do no harm to their patients. The true meaning of the oath had died with old Dr. Hippo.

So many toy lives were being destroyed. The Misleaders talked about the new health problems and how to "solve" them. Their solutions always involved some new and improved gummy pill. "If the first pill doesn't work, just add another one" was the motto of the pill factories and their representatives.

They were very pretty pills. They came in all shapes and sizes and in every color of the rainbow. Blue pills made you sleep, and red pills woke you up. Green pills took away the pain, and yellow pills made you feel happy.

One thing all the pills had in common was the profit they made the Misleaders. Not much was actually done to determine why the toys felt as they did. With all the resources, one would have thought the toys' illnesses could be cured. Yet, curing illness was never the goal. The Intele-tele instructed the toys to trust the science and even taught them what pills to ask for when visiting their doctors. All the while, the Misleaders funded the scientists and gave bonuses to the doctors for prescribing the "correct" treatments in the right amounts.

It was only roughly fifty years ago that toys trusted everything their doctors said. Doctors were trained professionals, dedicated to healing toys. Those were the good old days. Today with the Intele-tele and ToyNet, the toys had so much information at their fingertips. They could do their own research, which their busy doctors rarely had time to do, and work together for the best possible outcome.

Toys were assured repeatedly that the gummy pills they were being given weren't addicting. These gummy pills were designed by chemists and scientists and some of the most brilliant minds in the world, in some of the most state-of-the-art laboratories. Surely, they were safe to take.

And yet, it was clearly their addictive properties that made them so profitable. Pill plants funded most of the research to create new gummy pills, so designing new pills that cured disease opposed the goals of the corporation. Corporations had shareholders and stock prices to worry about. Billion-dollar babies were the goal of the pill creators. These were pills that toys would have to take every day for the rest of their lives. No pill plant would spend money to make pills the toys didn't need; they spent research funding to make pills toys couldn't live without.

"First you create the illness, then you create the treatment!" was one of Sir William Hates' famous quotes used at almost all pill plant motivational meetings.

The toys were losing their faith and unconditional trust in their doctors. Their doctors were being duped by the pill plants, and many toys knew it. The toys could not believe how long and how many lives it took for them to awaken to the fact that the pill plants caused the last epidemic that took so many lives. More lives had been taken by OxyCotton Candy than lost in the last toy war. Most toy doctors knew that there were alternative treatments, including nutritional counseling and physical therapy available for toys with back injuries, knee injuries, pulled muscles, chronic headaches, etc. Alternative treatments just weren't profitable and wouldn't get them any rewards from a pill plant. Besides, doctors' offices had to invest so much time to get the toy health security agencies to cover payment for them.

Gummy pills were quick, easy fixes. If a toy took too many pills, there were pills to reverse the effects of those pills. The Misleaders and the pill plants had collaborated to create the huge new stream of income that came from the reverse pills. They presented themselves as the heroes who were saving all those weak toys who had become addicted to their gummy pills.

Because toys were, by design, created to share happiness, sadness was unacceptable. Therefore, Happizac was created. It rapidly became a very popular pill, and many versions of Happizac were made. Even better, if Happizac didn't appear to be working, there was an add-on pill to increase the effect. No one really questioned how these gummies worked to create happiness, and it wouldn't have mattered if they did. No one knew. Oh yes, there were many scientific explanations provided on how Happizac possibly could work, but the *exact* mechanism wasn't known. There were warnings that came with the happy pill. Twenty-seven pill regulatory agencies warned it may cause psychosis, mania, suicidal ideation, violence, and homicidal ideation.

Purely by coincidence, it was after the release of Happizac and similar happy pills that there was a sharp increase in mass shootings and violence. The Misleaders quickly seized upon this crisis opportunity to lobby for gun control. It was guns that did the harm, not sick toys. Toy gun control laws would put an end to mass shootings!

Few posed the question, "How many of those shooters were taking happy pills"? It was finally discovered that sixty-five high-profile cases of mass shootings had been committed by individuals under the influence of these pills, yet there had been no planetary investigation into the link between senseless acts of violence and the use of mind-altering yum gummies.

A shooter named Magical Mouse was famous for his big ears, squeaky voice, and endearing personality. He wounded five at his high school while he was on happy pills. Ted, the fuzzy brown bear, had opened fire in a movie theater and killed twelve toys and wounded seventy others. At the time, he was under the care of a toy brain professional, but no information was released as to what gummy pills he was being given.

The doctors could not explain how a nonviolent toy given pills designed to create happiness suddenly became violent or suicidal. There were multiple cases of toys who had committed suicide days after starting to take the happy pills. There were so many old mommas and poppas who could tell their stories of what the pills had done to their toy children..

Even some of the Misleaders became afraid of what they were seeing. They introduced a bill that would require police to report certain crimes and suicides committed by toys using psychotropic pills, citing a large body of scientific research establishing a connection between violence and suicide and the use of those pills. Unfortunately, the bill stalled out. If the bill had passed, a reporting system would have been put into place to determine the extent to which violence is committed by those under the influence of mind-altering pills.

The true Misleaders and the pill plants could never allow this to happen. Eighty billion dollars a year was being made on happy pills alone. So, the media focus on gun control was ramped up. Pill plants media increased their campaigns to convince the masses that the happy pills were safe and effective. The Illuminators had Toy Planet in their clutches, so they introduced the true power of the Inoc.

Chapter 5

The Inocs

A nd as though the age of gummy pills wasn't enough, next came the Era of The Inocs. These were the injections administered from infancy through adulthood. The Misleaders had convinced the toy doctors and the toys that the poisonous, infection-filled childhood Inocs were so vital to the toys' health that the Misleaders had mandated their coverage by the health security agencies at no out-of-pocket cost to the toys. Many toys didn't know that the infections the Inocs were meant to prevent were grown on their own destroyed infant toys. In past years, the Inoc viruses had been grown on stuffed monkeys, but that had led to a disease that made the toys cells attack the toys themselves.

This was not a problem for the Misleaders until information had been leaked out by one of the "conspiracy" theory toys. It was the beginning of the anti-Inoc movement, and the Misleaders needed the toys to trust them. Inocs were now required for school entry with few exceptions. Most toy parents were made to feel ignorant if they questioned the Inoc laws and did not want their toy children to be ostracized or put at risk for some deadly disease. Many still "trusted the science" and those that were in power. They wanted their children to be safe even though in their hearts they knew something was deadly wrong.

So many parents were reporting their toy children were changing after they received their Inocs. It was the most powerful and wealthiest of the Misleaders, Sir William Hates, who talked the most about the importance of Inocs to eradicate all toy disease. This made the Inocs very profitable. Old Inocs were reformulated with higher costs. New ones were being introduced at unthinkable prices. The Inocs were way more profitable than the woody pill or the vital sign pill. The Misleaders were coming out with new Inocs faster than the toys could look up the diseases on ToyNet.

And yet, the results of Inocing all the toys were happening too slowly for the Illuminated toys. Something radical, on a grand scale, had to be done. A virus was created to do the trick. A virus that no one seemed to understand and that spread very quickly. They used worldwide propaganda to instill fear in all toys. They demanded toys stay in their homes and not expose themselves to others. They closed down toy businesses, toy schools, and toy houses of worship. The toy media played horrible scenarios of what *might* happen to the toys if the newly created virus was not controlled. Fear gripped Toy Planet. The effect of releasing the virus had just the effect the Illuminated toys wanted. The toys would do anything to get their lives back.

A new Inoc was created to combat the deadly virus. It was purely experimental because there was not time for safety testing. No government agency approval was necessary because this was an emergency. The misleaders had thought of everything. This included having Barrister TwistandSpin create a waiver the toys must sign agreeing to be part of the experiment. If anything went wrong, only the toy was liable. By signing the waiver, they had agreed, after all, to take all the risks involved.

There was a very courageous and caring doctor by the name of Dr. Brakefield. He tried to sound the alarm on what was happening with the Inocs. He had sat day after day listening to the heartbreaking stories of the parents of toys he had so diligently and compassionately tried to fix. He wasn't able to ignore the coincidences and commonalities between these injured toys. They had all had negative reactions to the Inocs. He was in disbelief when he was discredited as a toy doctor for his opinions. He had meticulously documented and presented overwhelming evidence on how many of these conditions could have been avoided.

Dr. Brakefield knew that public health officials were accepting a previously unknown burden of chronic disease, especially pervasive spectral disorder, autoimmune disorders, and developmental disorders. He was trying to put the brakes on some disconcerting practices being executed in the Inoc protocol. He had testified, offering compelling evidence of lower autism rates in unInoc'd populations vs. Inoc'd populations. These health histories signaled an urgent need to assess the acceptability of a "greater good" Inoc policy. The Center for Planet Disease Control was safeguarding its Inoc adverse reaction database statistics seemingly as tightly as national security secrets.

A true turning point for Dr. Brakefield was his patient Playa. He had cared after beautiful, adorable little baby Playa since she first left the toy factory. Playa's skin was so plush and soft you just wanted to cuddle her. Her cloth covering had a hint of pink, and her silk hair was wound in spiral curls. Her large glass eyes were an intense sparkling blue that made them hard not to stare into. Her small, puckered lips always had a soft laugh coming out of them that brought a smile onto anyone's face.

Playa was created perfect in every way. She was light as a feather when you held her in your arms and content to play by herself for hours on end. Baby Playa had met her "developmental milestones," such as crawling and walking, on schedule during her first eighteen months of life. However, two days after receiving four childhood Inocs during a routine wellness checkup, she developed a fever and became irritable and lethargic. The symptoms continued and worsened over the next few months. Her parents became worried about her language development and had her assessed.

The doctors concluded there were deficits in communication and social development. Playa had a persistent loss of previously acquired language, lacked eye contact, and no longer related well to others. She persistently screamed and arched her back. It was obvious the infant was suffering horrible pain. Dr. Brakefield concluded Playa was developmentally delayed and had pervasive features. He continued his research into the tummy biome and the connection it held to similar toys he had treated with this disorder. He knew there were ways to help and prevent this from happening. Unfortunately for perfect Playa, it was too late, she had to be medicated for the rest of her life.

Holly Jolly was as happy of a doll as she was beautiful. You pulled her string, and she would make you laugh. She was designed to comprehend what other toys would find humorous and loved bringing joy to these toys. It seemed after each time she had her Inocs, she found her role more difficult. She couldn't figure out why, so she went to visit Dr. Glow. Dr. Glow assured her he would be able to give her answers after they ran a perfectly safe dye through her toy body that would allow him to see her toy processing center more clearly.

The toys liked colorful dyes. They were dyed beautiful colors themselves. No one thought the dyes could hurt them. Holly Jolly had no idea that the dye was really a toxic metal. Holly Jolly was excited to feel better and think more clearly, so she went in for the test to get answers. The dye instantly made her feel hot, and her soft cotton stuffing burned from within. She was told that was a normal reaction from the dye and it would go away quickly.

It actually did not go away at all. Five years after the test, Holly Jolly was no longer able to make others laugh, and her skin still burned. Holly Jolly could no longer fulfill the purpose The I had created her for. It was a "**mystery**" to the Glow doctors who administered the toxic fluid. The dye was approved by all the healthcare agencies, so it had to be safe. Holly was never ever jolly again.

Dr Brakefield loved seeing the twins Mercury and Mars. He wished he had been their pediatrician and could have helped them to avoid their tragic outcome. Mercury was a soft, fully stuffed doll with stringy, fiery red hair. She and Mars were as close as any two siblings could be. Mercury took quite a liking to her **brother's** toys: trucks, cars, planes, and trains. He loved her dolls, kitchen sets, and baby stroller.

Mercury and Mars were inseparable morning, noon, and night. They would dance when music came on, hug and cuddle while Nannymom watched over them. The first time they were given their Inocs (five at the same time) they were four years old. The toy doctor had insisted that because they were so behind in their Inocs it would be fine to do these all in one visit, to get caught up on the recommended schedule. Only two days later, Mercury had a grand seizure.

By the time they got to the hospital, the seizure had already passed. Nannymom informed the doctors that she had just had her Inocs two days prior. The emergency doctor blamed a fever brought on by the Inocs for the seizure. Yet, Mercury had had no fever before or after the event. They were assured everything was fine and it shouldn't happen again. She was supposed to be healthy and happy, but she had another grand seizure the next day. She was hospitalized for two days, and Nannymom told every doctor that walked into Mercury's room that this started two days after her Inocs and she was sure that there was a correlation between the two.

Nannymom's concerns were just brushed off, Mercury's symptoms ignored and again passed off as a fever seizure. Still, there was no fever. Luckily, the next month came and went without any seizures. Nannymom was starting to think the doctors were right about the fever seizure. All was well again until it was time for more Inocs. The seizures started immediately. Mercury was put on a seizure pill and only had one seizure a month thereafter. Once again, Nannymom was reassured by the doctors that there couldn't possibly be a link between the Inocs and the seizures. Five months later, she received five more Inocs to stay on the recommended Inocs schedule. She had to catch up in order to attend toy preschool the upcoming year.

Within a month, Mercury was having two seizures a week and then three and then multiple seizures a day. It was heart-wrenching to see such a sweet doll in so much pain. Her family felt helpless. Mercury was no longer able to speak, even a babble. She would just moan in different pitches that were heart-wrenching to anyone who heard. Mars was too young to understand what was happening to his sister. He did not understand why she didn't want to play with the toy trains and planes anymore.

Nannymom was so mad at herself that she had trusted the doctors. She had been reassured over and over that everything was fine. Why didn't these doctors take the time to research how many of their toys' and families' lives were being changed forever.

Dr. Brakefield's and Nannymom's lives had been altered. Mercury's life change would not be in vain. Their mission now was to share the truth and all the stories of the toys who had been harmed to save the next generation of toys. Way too many toys were being damaged and not enough research was being done as to how or why.

Dr. Brakefield advocated for a safety-first Inoc program, not an anti-Inoc program. He was quite aware and very concerned that if something did not change, and change soon, pervasive spectral disorder would soon affect every toy family on Toy Planet. This was a mathematical certainty.

As with a deeply flawed string of studies reminiscent of the junk research once used to defend tobacco safety, science would dispel any of Dr. Brakefield's safety questions supported by research on his patients as being anti-Inoc. Once a doctor or a toy was labeled as anti-Inoc, they were now ostracized to the fringe of society. Anti-Inoc proponents were labeled radicals who didn't follow the science and who didn't care about toy health and safety.

Chapter 6

The Needle Had
Replace the Sword

A very wise old toy named Advocate Fella had grown up in a highly educated household. He was a member of a toyatarian political family. His mother always asked, "What good will you do for the world next?"

We all wonder what our purpose is in life, but sometimes we don't find it; it finds us. This was the case for Advocate Fella. He had started seeing broken toys brought into his office by their parents when he was a young advocate. These parents observed changes in their young toys after they were Inoc'd. Many symptoms happened immediately or seemingly overnight. He heard story after story of a previously social, loving, and happy child transforming into one who could no longer tolerate touch, make eye contact, and would scream, spin, and bang its head for no apparent reason. In all cases, the toy parents would try everything to comfort the suffering child, but to no avail. By the time the parents brought their child, or sometimes multiple children, to Advocate **Fella's** office, they had exhausted resources and themselves.

Many of the toy parents had turned raggedy even though it was not their original design. They had seen multiple doctors and been to multiple clinics and no one had any explanation for why their beloved toy had been so injured. One thing that all the doctors and nurses knew with certainty was that it was not caused by the Inocs. Inocs were safe and necessary for a healthy toy.

Advocate Fella was very bright and naturally curious. He continued observing how things were changing with the toys. He listened to all the toys and their stories as he worked on discovering the cause. He was not only concerned but also frightened by what he saw. There were so many seriously ill young toys, and this had never been the case before. There had been a few chronically ill young toys when he had started, but now it was an epidemic. What was happening to these young toys? Could it be from the Inocs? The medical symptoms differed from any he had ever seen. The affected toys didn't like to wear clothes, they complained of burning skin, many would hold their arms up to their sides, and some even flapped their tiny hands. Advocate Fella's purpose had found him. He had to determine what was happening with these toys and make it stop.

He began to research the Inoc industry. What was in the Inocs that could cause such a vast spectrum of symptoms? How many Inocs did a child receive? How much money was made from Inocs? This was an important one; he knew to always follow the money.

What he discovered was truly remarkable. When he had been a boy, he received four Inocs and was fully compliant with the Toy Health Organization guidelines on Inocs. At that time, children did not receive more than one shot in a single visit. In the next decade, another combined Inoc was added to the schedule. This one was designed to prevent the red spot illness and the lumpy neck illness. Child toys were Inoc'd against eight illnesses. Decades later, sixteen Inocs were required, with more recommended. Then it was twenty-four and currently it was seventy-two with hundreds more in the Inoc pipeline. Illnesses were combined into one prick, and many Inocs had to be administered repeatedly.

Despite this, no studies were being performed on the risk of combining or increasing the Inoc schedule. What were the effects of this many Inocs being injected into a toy? None of the pill plants or Misleaders were asking this vital question. It appeared few toys were even interested in knowing. It was a game of Inoc roulette! An open-ended experiment with no predictable outcome. In the early days of Inocs, there had already been children and adults falling ill from them. Some became paralyzed, and the lawsuits had begun. Parents knew it was the Inocs that had paralyzed their children.

Advocate Fella knew he was on to something. He dug deeper and found that the lawsuits had kept piling up over the decades, linking Inocs to illness and death. So much so that many of the manufacturers of Inocs had gone out of business. The Misleaders knew something drastic had to be done if they were going to continue their mission.

Therefore, The Toy Factory Inoc Injury Compensation Program was created. It was perfect. Damaged toys could no longer sue the manufacturers, regardless of their injuries. A

Misleader fund was created to pay damaged toys. But it got even better. First, toys had to get their doctors to report their injury into a highly confusing, time-consuming system. Most doctors did not wish to go to all that trouble, and besides, as Dr. Ostrich often pointed out, "There's no real proof the Inoc caused this."

Next, damaged toys would have to file a claim in the Misleader court and prove their damage was from an Inoc. And the true brilliance of the plan was that the toys would then receive compensation based on a set formula of injury. They even thought to put in a destroyed toy cap. If a toy was damaged beyond repair and had to be discarded, then the payout would be capped at $250,000. This was more than sufficient for the loss of a beloved toy. The Misleaders argued this point and won.

The effect of pill plant protection was dramatic. It skyrocketed from a million-dollar industry to a fifty-billion-dollar industry and twenty percent of all pill plant revenues. With this new money, hundreds of new Inocs were in the research pipeline. Much of the cost of Inocs was now covered by the Misleaders, who received a portion of all earned monopoly money from all toys earnings and shared some back with the pill plants. A pill plant's spokestoy, Squeaker, had guaranteed that. Squeaker was highly effective because he never allowed his voice to be silenced or drowned out. He was purposely created with a specialized speaker in his throat that made the sound of his voice so grating that no Misleader could refuse him. Adding to the effect, the message would replay over and over again.

Advocate Fella followed the money, and there was lots of it being made. But what about the link to all the illnesses? The toy doctors said it wasn't possible, but was that true when there were one hundred and fifty possible afflictions listed on each Inoc package insert? These package inserts were never actually given to the toy patients, so few toys were aware of the incredible risk involved in receiving Inocs.

Advocate Fella had eleven brothers and sisters as well as three girl toys and three boy toys of his own. He had over forty-five cousins. He had gathered data from his family and consenting toys and their families whom he had represented. Advocate Fella had been collecting data for thirty years now. He had seen afflictions become common that had truly been rare in past decades. Chronic afflictions such as developmental illness, focus disorders, language delay, speech delay, tics, immunity disorders, food allergies, and the most widespread, pervasive spectral disorder, a lifetime sentence of dependency and suffering in silence for a beautiful toy child.

Advocate Fella did not claim all new afflictions were caused by Inocs, yet it could not be a mere coincidence. The precise timing of the Inoc schedule and the elevated levels of aluminum and mercury injected into the toys changed. Later, the amount was tripled and then quadrupled. Researchers found that the maximum exposure from Inocs in the first six months of life was 187.5 micrograms of mercury. That number far exceeded the amount considered safe by any of the toy protection agencies.

The typical two-month Inoc schedule injected a whopping 62.5 micrograms of mercury. That amount equaled one hundred twenty-five times the limit of what the toy protection agencies declared was safe. Could these toxins be related to the many afflictions? Advocate Fella pondered and researched and scratched his chin. Upon doing a ToyNet search, he quickly found several hundred studies linking mercury to toy wiring shorts and ailments that caused the toy body to attack itself. All participants in the earliest toy study done in 1930 expired and had to be thrown into the discarded toy bin. Mercury poisoning caused sensitivity to light, rashes, sensitive skin or a burning sensation on the skin, emotional volatility, insomnia, and problems with social interaction. The symptoms of mercury poisoning and pervasive spectral disorder had a great deal of overlap.

Advocate Fella set up a meeting with the Misleader leader, Elephant. There was too much evidence to be ignored. Irreparable harm was being done to the toys on a grand scale. Elephant was gracious enough to take the meeting. He had gone on record in the past, stating his concern over Inocs being linked to pervasive spectral disorder. He went as far as to say that the massive combined Inocs were the very cause of pervasive spectral disorder to newly created toys. He said he personally knew newly created toys who had been damaged. Besides, he couldn't be seen as slighting the famous Advocate Fella. He had a history of friendship with Fella's influential family and did not wish to offend anyone with that much power and influence, until someone with greater power and influence came along.

Advocate Fella wasted no time when he finally got face-to-face with Elephant. "Elephant, you are aware that the pill plants are creating Inocs laced with dangerous toxins, immune response boosters, and preservatives. Even Leader Jackass can tell you that. The four pill plants that produce all seventy-two Inocs that are mandated for the toys have committed crimes against the toys. In the last decade, those four pill plants have collectively paid thirty-five billion dollars in criminal penalties, damages, and fines for untruth, fabricating stories, paying the doctors to lie, and promoting lies to toy doctors that killed toys. The toys know they can't sue the pill plants for Inoc damage, and the Pill Plants know they are safe from any repercussions. There is no incentive for them to do extensive safety testing and ensure no harm will come to the pricked toys. Attorney Twistthetruth has done a wonderful job spinning the Inoc message. That's why the pill plant has greatly multiplied its production of Inocs beginning in 1989. They have no incentive to make Inocs safe, other than to protect the trusting toys, which obviously isn't the goal."

Puppet leader Elephant knew when to lose his memory and how to agree and disagree at the same time. He had played this game often. He put on his "I'm truly concerned" face and said, "Fella, I would like you to chair a commission to review Inoc safety. You obviously came to me because you are aware of my genuine, heartfelt personal convictions about this very important issue. I am honored you are including me in this matter."

Advocate Fella left that meeting with great hope for the future of Inoc safety. For months after this meeting, he met with Elephant's team, devising a plan as to what the new commission would look like. Oddly, he never heard another word from

Misleader Elephant himself. It was only after much time had passed that he was told, "The Stuffed Elephant administration has decided to go in another direction." Coincidentally, all the Misleaders were now heavily invested in the pill plants. The Puppet Masters celebrated this victory. The dangled carrots had once again succeeded. Advocate Fella felt betrayed; he had fallen for Elephant's feigned sincerity. He was disappointed Elephant had succumbed to the greed, power, and authority of the pill plants and their representatives.

Advocate Fella was aware most toys were oblivious to the fact that the pill plants that made the Inocs had this very important exemption. The Misleaders had created an exemption from safety testing Inocs in the event of an emergency that they intended to create. In fact, Inocs were the only product made at the pill plants that did not have to be tested for safety under these conditions. The Inoc exemption program was implemented as a national security defense against biological attack, placed under the guise that they wanted to make sure they could get Inocs out to the public quickly if any new infectious disease was created that threatened Toy Planet. They wanted to remove all the regulatory hinderances that would prevent quick deployment of the Inocs. They had found a way to overcome the "nonsense," as

Grandfather Neverenuph trusted they would. Inocs could now be made mandatory.

The toys had too many decisions to make in their simple lives as it was. Voluntary Inocs forced these simple-minded toys to do research and read information their unscientific minds couldn't possibly comprehend. The Misleaders counted on the "sheep" to want to be told what was best for them and their newly created toys.

All the written research on Inocs was so technical; it could have been explained in simpler terms but what would be the point of that? Most toys didn't wish to waste their time researching what was being injected into them. Once all Inocs were mandatory, there would be no reason to question. The Misleaders counted on this, and it worked. History had reverted its course, and for the Fourth Realm to succeed again, tragically, experiments would be done on toys, which would lead to their ultimate demise.

The Puppet Masters now had Misleader figureheads at every level of toy factories in every toy and to insure they couldn't be hindered by regulations that would curtail their profits or their plan. This was not a conventional war over control of Toy Planet as they had fought in the past; rather, this was a war being waged in the shadows so that no toy knew who their enemy truly was. This enemy didn't march out onto a battlefield with courage.

This enemy hid behind veils of deception and layers of lies.

The trusting toys weren't questioning that no one could or wished to share the actual risk of combining so many Inocs in the newly created toys. There was no research on the effects of continually adding new Inocs to the schedule, even though scientists knew that combining the immune boosters and preserves was not the safest way to protect the toys, but it was the most cost effective.

No one had an answer for the few toys who did dare question the short-term and long-term effects of this Inoc experiment. Scientists would not even guarantee the Inocs would save more lives than they would take or benefit more than they would harm. In truth, all scientific evidence that did prove this was either destroyed or debunked as untrue. Huge budgets were put in place to spread pro-Inoc propaganda and to buy any scientific researcher that proved Inocs posed a risk. They were attempting to mandate Inocs for the toys with no clue of the risks involved.

The safety testing that was being done was more for show than science. The subjects used to test the anti-paralysis Inoc were only observed for forty-eight hours after being pricked. The effects of the liver Inoc now being given to every new toy on its day of creation were only observed for five days during safety testing. If the toy expired, or became defective on day six, this data wasn't integrated into the research and no changes were necessary. It was as if it had never happened. If any toy later attained food allergies, developed pervasive spectral disorder, became immunocomprised, etc., it never happened according to science. They could say it was safe.

Oddly, there was one Inoc, the red spot Inoc, that was one of the earliest developed that had no safety testing listed on its package insert. For many years, troubled Advocate Fella asked, Where was it? Why didn't safety data exist? It weighed on him so heavily that Advocate Fella brought legal action to the Misleaders, demanding to know where this data was.

The pill plants eventually released the safety testing data that was performed. The research was completed on eight hundred toys. This was odd. Normal standard testing would have been done on at least twenty thousand toys. This Inoc would eventually be injected into billions of toys. The safety testing lasted only forty-two days and showed fifty percent of the toys participating in the trial developed serious adverse reactions. These included fever, headache, atypical red spot illness, nausea, vomiting, anaphylaxis, encephalitis, seizures, convulsion, and asthma. This Inoc, according to its own studies, caused worse illness than the red spots it was originally pretending to prevent.

Upon receiving this information, Advocate Fella was more determined than ever. He was not going to go down without a fight. He knew the toys had a right to know what was being injected into their bodies and the possible results. He made sure this information got out on ToyNet, the Intele-tele, and even wrote a story for the toys so they could understand it.

Toys started to be anti-Inoc even though Advocate Fella himself was not anti-Inoc. He could see the benefits of Inocs if done safely and if the toys were treated as uniquely as they truly were. He knew all toys were special and different and would not all have the same response to the Inocs. A simple solution was available. Test the toys for individual differences and make sure they were healthy before receiving an Inoc. No sick or weak toy should ever be given an Inoc, nor any toy with a family history of bad Inoc reactions. Dr. Dolittle knew this. Everyone ignored it, but his first priority was keeping them on the schedule to achieve optimal Inoc rates according to the health security agencies. Optimal rates meant optimal monopoly money for Dr. Dolittle and his colleagues. The health of the pig banks was more vital than the toys' health.

Advocate Fella wanted to do the right thing for the toys. He wanted the Misleaders to be forthcoming with all the Information he knew they had, and he wanted all testing performed by scientists outside of the pill plants because pill plant scientists were paid to do research that benefitted them. Objectivity was not their job.

Another simple, commonsense item Advocate Fella thought was necessary and more than reasonable would be an adverse reaction reporting system that was easy for doctors to use. He recommended that they start by having every parent give feedback at thirty days, sixty days, and ninety days after every Inoc given. He also suggested that Inocs not be given to toys who already had a sibling with pervasive spectral disorder.

Safety first and do no harm was what mattered in medicine, right?

Based on all the research from the Planet Health Organization, Advocate Fella knew that Inocs given one at a time had a much less likely chance of damaging a precious toy. But most importantly, it should be the toy's decision. Inocs must remain a choice, because while The I had created all toys equal, it did not mean that all toys were created the same. Each toy was created with different cellular make-up, chips, processors, functioning systems, and defense systems that affected how it would respond to the combination of toxins and infections found in Inocs.

Advocate Fella didn't trust the foxes to guard the chicken coop. He believed Inocs should be heavily regulated by independent agencies, researchers, and Inoc-concerned organizations outside of the pill plants and the Misleaders' authority. The Misleaders could not be trusted to be objective because the pill plants were their biggest source of monopoly money. They got greedier and greedier and less ethical by the day.

The Puppet Masters had guaranteed that the Misleaders would do whatever it took to keep up the mass enforcement of Inocs. Any toy who stood in the way of their goals or questioned the Great Reject had to be censored and silenced. They created derogatory labels to be used in their propaganda campaigns, so any toy questioning the safety of an Inoc was an anti-Inoc conspiracy theorist.

This included Advocate Fella. He, along with other Inoc freedom-of-choice advocates, was portrayed as crazy and irrational and the fringe of toy society. The Misleaders did not want a debate on Inoc safety. They prevented the masses of toys from looking at any science or statistics that mattered. One in fifty toys had pervasive spectral disorder, and fifty percent of all young toys were chronically damaged; the Misleaders didn't want to hear those facts or speak to the fact that many toys had to be disposed of in the toy bin after receiving an Inoc.

The rate of pervasive spectral disorders was increasing at alarming rates, but the Misleaders kept claiming not to know why. The pill plants ignored all stories brought forth by the parents of these permanently affected children. Film documentaries featuring whistleblowers' tales of millions of toys who had been negatively affected were silenced. The Misleaders were sure to censor and remove any data or information that contradicted the Great Reject.

It was easy for them because they owned and controlled all the toy media. They used their widespread influence to divide those choosing to Inoc and those who refused. They used fear to turn the toys against each other. Some truth still reached the toys by those who were willing to sacrifice their own reputations and monopoly money to save their fellow toys. There would always be those martyrs and do-gooders that were a thorn in the sides of the Illuminated toys striving toward an enlightened society. It was these few that couldn't be bought or shamed, that stood between the toy masses and their toy masters. They put billions of monopoly money every year into advertising, not only selling gummy pills and Inocs but also dividing those who were choosing not to Inoc and those who were. It was also quite mysterious that the toy doctors who spoke out against the Inocs would disappear or die suddenly in freak accidents. Anyone who spoke out about what was happening within the pill plants and regulatory agencies would be fired and removed from their positions immediately.

The Institute of Wellness represented the ultimate authority on Inoc safety. The Institute had reported one hundred-fifty known afflictions believed to be caused by The Inocs and directed Misleaders to study them. They were asked in 1994; they refused. They were asked again in 2011; they refused. They were asked every year since, but always refused with no repercussions.

The final obstacle standing between the pill plants and injured toys were the toy parents. Pill plants could not tolerate toy parents who even hinted at not Inocing their toys. The propaganda message was clear: There is no such thing as Inoc injury. It was all an illusion and those parents who had broken toys were just hysterical and delusional, grasping for anything to blame. These parents and their advocates were a threat to toymanity.

The Iluminated used the media to let those on Toy Planet know these toys were not just anti-Inoc, they were anti-society. They posed a threat to every toy on the planet. These toys must be contained for safety reasons, hence the implementation of the Inoc passport. No toy would be allowed to travel, visit public sites, attend school, worship The I, or have gainful employment unless they had their Inoc passport to prove they cared for their fellow toys. These anti-Inoc toys must be ostracized from society for being the enemy. Toy Planet had now reached a critical point in its history. There were currently more defective toys than functional toys. Toys now related to each other by their defects. Defect communities, representing each and every toy defect, could be joined on ToyNet.

Advocate Fella was beyond frustrated. He and a team of scientists and doctors began sharing information and forming alliances. The Intele-tele, ToyNet, Wokey-talkies and Squeaky Toy Media were censoring and discrediting every attempt made to tell the truth. The irony was the near impossibility of sharing or obtaining information in a world connected by communication devices. There were now few ways to warn the toys of what was happening. It was becoming more and more difficult to publish or speak the truth. There was an entire army of bots launched on ToyNet to post false information and belittle those posting any messages contrary to the Illuminated's plan. The bots were also launched to remove all studies that proved Inocs unsafe. Any anti-Inoc searches would be automatically redirected to pro-Inoc propaganda.

The toy masses had to believe that the majority agreed in the new enlightened society. The Illuminated needed the toys that intuitively sensed something was terribly wrong to feel that they were alone. They could not allow these toys to unite. The elite knew the true power lay with the toys themselves. History had taught them that truth will spread like wildfire if the first spark was not extinguished. No one appeared to be questioning who was behind the censoring of information. The toys were aware they were being censored and the Intele-tele blamed those who ran ToyNet. But who were they answering to?

Chapter 7

The Erosion of Freedom

The Illuminated couldn't believe how smoothly it was going, like skating on ice. It was laughable how quickly they had been able to change toy society. Overnight, most toys accepted the new normal. In one year, from the release of the lab-created contagion, many of them had watched their profits soar. The toys began lining up and Inocing as fast as they could. They would be pricked with an Inoc that was experimental with little safety testing. An Inoc that wasn't even an Inoc by its very definition. They happily signed consent forms agreeing to be guinea pigs in a worldwide experiment. The largest in history. That's what the Intel-tele told them to do. Millions of toys would be damaged and broken as the outcome. Wealthcare had become their reality.

No one was even suspicious when they targeted toys who received aid from the Misleaders. The propaganda message clearly stated it was to protect the most vulnerable of the population. Vintage toy soldiers, toys who had lost their marbles, toys that had slow microprocessors, antique toys, and toy villains. If the Misleaders' goal was to eliminate much of the population, where would they begin? There were whispers they would sterilize the generation of young toys. How many toys did they intend to eliminate? There was no doubt the planet was crowded. It was a challenge to feed them all. Sir William Hates had hinted at the dire need for population elimination and a reduced population growth.

The one-percenters involved in the Great Reject had solidified their power around the world. They were raking in massive amounts of monopoly money and literally purchasing Toy Planet. All previous laws forbidding monopoly corporations were ignored. Soon there would be no more mom and pop shops; they were being forced to close by the Misleaders while the monopolized corporations guzzled up their market share. All independence would soon disappear. Dreams and goals belonged to independent thinking toys, not the new re-programmed toys. Many toys could not accept the transition and threw themselves into the discarded toy bin.

Toy Planet was unrecognizable post-contagion. The vintage toys recognized this for what it was: another HollowCost. They had survived the first and could see the blatant similarities. The Third Realm had implemented some of the very techniques being used by the Fourth Realm.

1. **Control of the media**

2. **Propaganda to spread their message**

3. **Burning books had changed to banning books**

4. **Experimentation of unwilling toys was now experimentation of unwitting toys**

5. **Report your neighbor became call the HOTLINE and report anyone not in compliance**

6. **Rewriting history to fit their ultimate view of society**

7. **Persecution of all who rebel**

8. **Banning faith and not allowing gathering in worship**

9. **Banning gun ownership**

10. **Restricting the right to travel**

11. Turning youth against their parents

12. Limiting freedom of speech and censorship of everything said

13. Control over educational content/programming

The outcome of this was a radically changed society. Toys were now going without necessary preventive healthcare while hospitals and doctors' offices were nearly empty. Elderly toys were forced to perish alone and be thrown in the discarded toy bin with no loved ones present. Toys in distress were separated from their families. Young toys lost a year of classroom education and only had access to the Misleader-controlled curriculum, which had been infused with divisive content and further widened the gap between the love the toys had once had for one another.

All toys were forced to isolate and live in fear. All social interaction and the joy it brought were forbidden. Concerts, sports, weddings, funerals, worship, classrooms, dining out, etc. were banned. There was an obvious double standard between the ruling class and the populace. The ruling class continued to travel and dine-out, their children attended classroom learning, and the businesses they owned were open.

Masks were required on all toys' faces, so smiles and emotions could not be shared. It was a mute world. The only feelings being shared were anger, hate, fear, and frustration. Toys now spent hour upon hour watching the Intel-tele and staring at their Wokey-talkies as the planet around them morphed to no longer resemble that which they had known. Inside, they were terrified how it was all going to end. The transformation was truly happening at warp speed. The nightmare that had been envisioned long before on that cold night in that cold castle with very cold hearts many years before was now reality. Nannymom had suffered many avertible losses since that night in that dark castle where she had served syrupy sodas while eavesdropping on the Illuminated as they outlined their plan, never comprehending how it would affect her so personally as she went about just doing her job. How totally helpless she had felt as Mercury's life was whisked away from her, how her dreams for Mercury were stolen one Inoc at a time. Painfully and horrendously helpless, she watched her darling Alfred Nickelsworth, her lifetime companion, die alone. He lay in a bed, only able to video chat his last words. Robbed of having his hand held, his head kissed, or a whisper in his ear, "Goodbye, my love."

How had they for one second agreed to any of this? The mission had come full circle. There was no more liberty for the masses of toys. The motto of the elite—Let no crisis go to waste––had proved advantageous once again.

Toy Planet had reached its tipping point. There was not one crisis but continual crises that were being created to keep the toys in a state of chaos and fear. Toys were being paid to march and burn down toy communities. Toy security agencies were being defunded. Random toy destruction was on the rise. The toys knew they could no longer trust the ruling class Misleaders, for they had led them toward destruction. The only answer was turning back to The I and His core values, as stated in the Toy Anthem.

Do no harm to one another. Love your sister and your brother.

No killing and no wars. Use your gifts and do your chores.

Toys don't judge, only love. We protect all gifts from above.

Knowledge is completely free. Sharing is what toys do for thee.

Telling lies is taboo. Toys don't lie. Toys love you.

All toys would have to join together to reverse what had been so quickly implemented to destroy their dreams and lives.

Stuffed Eagle Land housed three hundred and twenty-eight million toys. The toys far outnumbered the handful of Misleaders who had turned against them. Beginning with her own voice, Nannymom would be heard. They would no longer be masked, muffled, muted, or silenced in fear of persecution. They would not tolerate being isolated and divided. They would no longer bow down to the fictional politically correct movement. They would enforce the toyatarian code and remember why it was written in the first place. This would be a war waged without violence, a war that came from a place of love for all toys. They might not have the money or resources to fight the pill plants and the Misleaders, but they had The I, the truth, and love on their side. This would become known as a pinnacle turning point in toy history. It was a re-birth of Toy Planet and a return to life as The I had perfectly created it.

With the knowledge and influence of Advocate Fella, a plan had been devised to lead the toys back to health. Nannymom had been a member of the Toys Health Defense and National Inoc Information Center for quite a while, and she had joined their efforts to quell the lies, spread the truth, and save the toys. It was simple but would take sacrifice and commitment from all the toys.

1. Toys everywhere must demand that labs creating new illnesses be shut down immediately. The toys who protected these labs or where they were housed needed to be banished from society. No toy should have any dealings with these evildoers.

2. All toys must seek the truth for themselves and their loved ones. They must not trust the word of the Misleaders and their science.

3. The toys must create their own Inoc damage reporting system and directly report all adverse reactions to each other on this site. All negative reactions must be recorded, regardless of the amount of time passed from receiving the Inoc. The current reporting system was only capturing one percent of the actual destruction of toys. Everyone must share their stories to protect young toys and provide the research necessary to save them.

4. Toys must repeatedly contact the Misleaders in their area and demand these changes be made.

   a. Inocs must be made voluntary only.

   b. Masks must only be voluntary.

5. Toys must demand their right to toy guns and self-protection against those who would harm them and rule over them unjustly.

6. Toys must boycott monopolized corporations, so they lose their power.

7. Toys must not buy anything from Toy countries or companies that aren't toyitarian.

8. Toys must fiercely resist their voices being censored and boycott any website, social group, or company attempting to do so. They must resist any attempt to limit information sharing.

9. Toys must not allow themselves to be divided against each other. They must unite for the love of all toys.

10. Toys must stop supporting the pig banks and support small local banks and credit unions in their communities.

11. Toys must turn back to The I and away from the Inteletele and ToyNet.

Advocate Fella launched a website to encourage the toys to gather on ToyNet. All information and ideas about how to regain liberty could be shared. The toys were the only ones who could tell the truth and change the trajectory. It was up to the toys to reveal the truth. All toys were encouraged to start reporting adverse reactions.

Toy doctors who had been given the huge responsibility to protect the sanctity of life, who had taken an oath to do no harm, would have to stand up one by one and share the truth. They could not follow in the steps of the HollowCost doctors who were complicit with the Third Realm. They must share what they were seeing and do what was BEST for their patients. They must not bow down to the interest of pill plants. Last, they must continue to educate themselves in how to provide true health and wellness.

Only then would Nannymom find peace and create a better future for all the grandtoys.

In Conclusion

This book is a fairy tale for my grandchildren. I believe life can be a fairy tale if we choose to create and plan our lives as though we are writing our own story or making our own movie. I want them to have great expectations for themselves, as I have for them. I hope to inspire them, encourage them to build a good moral foundation for their lives, see their dreams come true (even if not from this world), and most importantly, have them experience happy, healthy, productive lives. They are beautiful and perfect, as we were all created. They fill my heart with joy and bring me smiles and laughter. If I can help them avert from plummeting into those potholes in the road that I failed to avoid, I will have accomplished a great deal.

We are all born with a purpose in life, yet when we ignore our inner voice and guidance system and succumb to negative influences, we will suffer the negative consequences. I pray they choose with the intent of achieving their higher purpose and bringing forth the lives they truly deserve. By choosing to live in darkness, we deny being all that we were meant to be. As we travel on the road of life, many signs can steer us toward light, and many signs steer us towards the darkness. One must not only look for these signs but also take heed to their message.

We must not clothe ourselves in a veil that casts shadows on all the good that is there for us. When we let go of our dreams and don't use all the talents and gifts we have been given, we give up our power and our light and therefore our own happiness. You must always claim the best life and listen to that voice inside, your gift, your compass to your true happiness. That voice says you can make a difference for yourself and for others. Please don't silence your voice through alcohol, drugs, marijuana, toxins in our food, toxic environments, and toxic people. I pray you don't detour down these paths of destruction and away from well-being and happiness. So many of your idols and mentors in life will do just that.

You will encounter many paths that no one set out to take: alcoholism, drug addiction, vaping, food addictions, pornography. Recognize them as paths that lead away from joy. No one wanted to wallow or get stuck in these destructive addictions. Making a bad choice a few times can quickly become a bad habit. We are all capable of viewing individuals with self-destructive habits, seeing the tremendous pain these habits have caused themselves and others, and still head on their heels right down that road after them. Many are fooled into thinking they will be the one who never gets addicted, but so often they are wrong. Many substances today are designed to be addicting. You will lose the battle sooner or later. The odds are stacked, and most definitely not in your favor. I pray something in my words on these pages resonates and permeates within you. I hope something says, "STOP, do not go there!" Choose wisely.

The I will be watching over you to guide and protect you from the Misleaders. And be assured, you are being misled. Those you were taught to admire and trust are causing you and the ones you love harm. You are allowed to question the science. It's your body and your mind and your children. You are entitled to educate yourself and ask questions, not offer blind trust. Study for yourself. Read for yourself. The information is available to make healthy choices for yourself. Love and admire what The I made you to be. You are not less than anyone else; you are equal. When that voice inside warns you that something is not right for you or your loved one, pay attention. The spirit is your inner guidance system.

Follow your dreams. Do not be tempted by instant gratification and bewitching friends who appear to be what you wish to be. Be you because you are the only one of you there is, and that is amazing! Choose to shine light in this very dark world. There will be many who need you to share your light with them. Be willing to truly stand out and stand ALONE in your beliefs. All the greatest individuals in history were willing to stand alone in their convictions, and in doing so, they bettered the lives of countless others.

Don't let Satan blow it out! Say, "I'm gonna let it shine!"

I hope you look at the world not as it is but start asking why it is as it is. How you can make it better?

Treat your body as your temple; it is the seat of the soul.

Love God.

Love yourself.

Love one another.

RESOURCES FOR INFORMATION AND REPORTING

www.nvic.org/reporting-system.aspx

childrenshealthdefense.org/